The Jewel Fairies

For Danni who loves fairies

Special thanks to
Narinder Dhami

ORCHARD BOOKS

First published in Great Britain in 2005 by Orchard Books
This edition published in 2018 by The Watts Publishing Group

1 3 5 7 9 10 8 6 4 2

© 2018 Rainbow Magic Limited.
© 2018 HIT Entertainment Limited.
Illustrations © Georgie Ripper 2005

HiT entertainment

A CIP catalogue record for this book is available from the British Library.

ISBN 978 1 40834 872 7

Printed in Great Britain by Clays Ltd, Elcograf S.p.A.

MIX
Paper from
responsible sources
FSC® C104740
FSC
www.fsc.org

The paper and board used in this book are made from wood from responsible sources

Orchard Books
An imprint of Hachette Children's Group
Part of The Watts Publishing Group Limited
Carmelite House, 50 Victoria Embankment, London EC4Y 0DZ

An Hachette UK Company
www.hachette.co.uk
www.hachettechildrens.co.uk

India
the Moonstone
Fairy

by Daisy Meadows

illustrated by Georgie Ripper

Join the Rainbow Magic Reading Challenge!

Read the story and collect your fairy points to climb the Reading
Rainbow online. Turn to the back of the book for details!

This book is worth 5 points.

Adventure
Playground

Tippington
Manor

Tippington
Town

The Tall
Toy
Store

Fountain

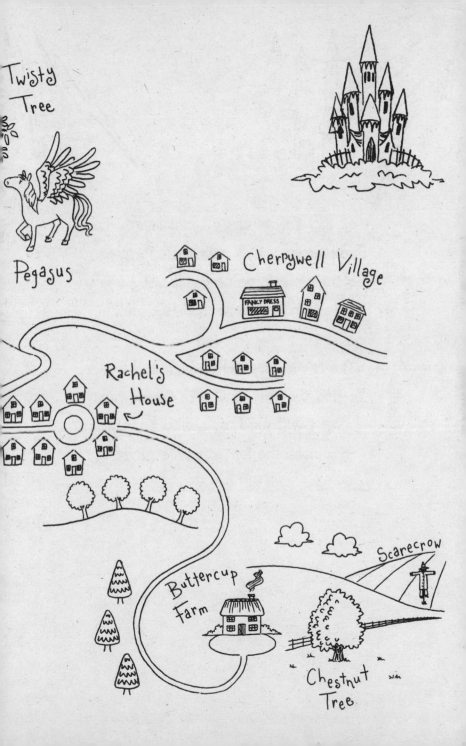

Twisty Tree

Pegasus

Cherrywell Village

FANCY DRESS

Rachel's House

Buttercup Farm

Scarecrow

Chestnut Tree

By Frosty magic I cast away
These seven jewels with their fiery rays,
So their magic powers will not be felt
And my icy castle shall not melt.

The fairies may search high and low
To find the gems and take them home.
But I will send my goblin guards
To make the fairies' mission hard.

Contents

A Nasty Nightmare

"Kirsty, help!" Rachel Walker shouted. "The goblins are going to get me!"

Panting, Rachel glanced behind her. She was running as fast as she could, but the green goblins were getting closer and closer. They were grinning nastily, showing their pointed teeth. Now one of them had grabbed Rachel by the

shoulder, and was shaking her hard—

"Rachel?" Kirsty Tate was leaning over her friend's bed, shaking her awake. "Wake up! You're having a nightmare."

Rachel woke and sat up in bed. "What time is it?" she asked. "I dreamt that there were horrible goblins chasing me, and I couldn't escape."

"It's 7.30," Kirsty replied, perching on the edge of the bed. "Why were the goblins after you?"

Rachel frowned. "I can't remember," she sighed. "But you know what, Kirsty? I've got a funny feeling that Jack Frost might be up to something again!"

Kirsty's eyes opened wide. "Oh, do you really think so?" she gasped. "Then maybe our fairy friends will need our help!"

Rachel and Kirsty shared a magical secret. They had become friends with the fairies, and whenever there was a problem in Fairyland, Kirsty and Rachel were called on to help.

The fairies' greatest enemy was Jack Frost. He was always looking for ways to make trouble, helped by his mean goblin servants. Not long ago, Jack Frost had tried to ruin the celebration party for King Oberon and Queen Titania's 1000th jubilee. But luckily, Kirsty and Rachel had come to the rescue.

"We'll have to keep our eyes open," Rachel agreed. "If the fairies need our help, they'll let us know somehow."

Kirsty nodded. "Well, it's only the beginning of half-term, and I'm staying with you for the whole week," she pointed out. "So we have plenty of time."

Before Rachel could reply, the sweet, tinkling sound of music suddenly filled the room. Both Kirsty and Rachel jumped.

"What's that?" Kirsty asked.

Rachel looked puzzled for a moment,
but then she began to laugh. "It's my
music box!" she smiled, pointing at
the dressing-table. "The one the Party
Fairies gave us."

After helping the Party Fairies to
stop Jack Frost from spoiling the jubilee
celebrations, Rachel and Kirsty had
each been given a beautiful, musical
jewellery box with a tiny model
fairy on top. Rachel's box sat on her
dressing-table, and the girls could see
that the fairy was spinning round in
time to the music.

"Yes, but how
did it start up
on its own?"
Kirsty asked,
with a frown. "I
didn't wind it,
and you've only
just woken up."

"Look!"
Rachel gasped. "The box is glowing!"

Rachel scrambled out of bed, and she and Kirsty rushed over to take a closer look. Rachel was right. The box was glowing with a faint pink light which shone from under the closed lid.

"Lift the lid, Rachel," Kirsty whispered.

Hardly daring to breathe, Rachel reached out and slowly lifted the lid.

Immediately a glittering shower of multi-coloured fairy dust burst from the jewellery box. It swirled around the girls, wrapping them in a cloud of sparkles and lifting them off their feet.

Fairy News

After just a moment or two, the sparkles began to drift away and the girls felt their feet lightly touch the ground. Rachel and Kirsty blinked a few times and looked around.

"Kirsty, we're in Fairyland!" Rachel gasped.

"In our pyjamas!" Kirsty added.

The girls were now fairy-sized with glittering fairy wings on their backs, and they were standing in the golden Great Hall of the fairy palace. King Oberon, Queen Titania and a small crowd of fairies stood in front of them. The girls noticed that they all looked worried.

Queen Titania stepped forwards. "You are very welcome, girls," she said with a smile. "I hope you don't mind us bringing you here so unexpectedly."

"Of course not," Rachel said quickly.

"You have been such good friends to us in the past," the Queen went on, "that we were hoping we could call on you again, now that we are in trouble."

"What's wrong?" asked Kirsty anxiously.

"Let me explain," the Queen replied sadly. "Every year, at Halloween, we have a huge celebration in Fairyland. All the fairies have to recharge their fairy magic for another year."

"So every fairy in Fairyland parades around the Grand Square," King Oberon put in. "Then they all march into the palace to a very special chamber, where Queen Titania's tiara rests upon a velvet cushion."

"It sounds wonderful," Rachel sighed, hoping that she and Kirsty might be allowed to watch the grand procession one day.

Queen Titania nodded. "It is," she replied. "And my tiara is very important for fairy magic. It has seven beautiful jewels set in it. A sparkling fountain of fairy dust pours from each of the seven jewels, and they join together to form one great, glittering rainbow of magical fairy dust."

Kirsty and Rachel were listening carefully, their eyes wide.

"What happens then?" Kirsty asked.

"Each fairy must dip her wand in the rainbow fountain to recharge it," the Queen explained. "Then she will be able to perform magic for another year."

The King shook his head sadly. "But now Jack Frost has put a stop to all that," he sighed. "Two nights ago, he crept into the palace and stole the seven jewels from the Queen's tiara!"

"Oh, no!" Rachel and Kirsty exclaimed together.

"Our special celebration was to take place in a week's time," the Queen went on, looking worried. "So the fairies' magic is already running low."

"The jewels must be returned to the tiara," King Oberon added, "before the fairies run out of the jewels' magic completely!"

"Does this mean that there will be no magic at all left in Fairyland?" asked Kirsty anxiously.

"Not exactly," the Queen replied. "Fairy magic isn't quite as simple as that. Some kinds of magic, like Weather Magic and Rainbow Magic, aren't controlled by the jewels."

22

"But the jewels do control some of the most important kinds of fairy magic," the King explained. "Like flying, wishes and sweet dreams. Some people have already started to have nightmares."

Rachel nodded, thinking of her own scary dream. "We have to get the jewels back!" she said firmly.

"Where is Jack Frost now?" Kirsty wanted to know. "Has he taken the jewels to his ice castle?"

The Queen shook her head. "Jack Frost doesn't have the jewels any more," she said. "Come with me, and I will show you what happened."

Rachel and Kirsty followed the
fairies outside into the beautiful
palace gardens. They
stopped beside the
golden pool, its
surface as clear and
smooth as glass.

"Look," Queen
Titania said
softly, waving
her wand over
the water.

Immediately
tiny ripples began
to spread across the
surface of the pool.
The ripples grew bigger and
bigger, and slowly a picture
appeared on the water's surface.

"It's Jack Frost!" Rachel exclaimed. Tall, thin, spiky Jack Frost stood in front of Queen Titania's golden tiara upon its velvet cushion. The seven magic jewels glittered as dazzling streams of magic dust poured from each one. Laughing, Jack Frost thrust his snowflake-tipped wand into the magic rainbow fountain, where it glowed like fire. "He is recharging his magic," the King explained.

Kirsty and Rachel watched in dismay as Jack Frost then prised the sparkling gems from the golden tiara. He waved his wand and immediately the jewels were encased in solid ice.

"What is he doing?" Rachel asked, puzzled.

"The light and heat of the jewels' magic makes them difficult for cold, icy creatures like Jack Frost and his goblins to hold," Queen Titania explained. "Look."

Now Jack Frost was whizzing back to his ice castle, carried by a frosty wind which blew him along. He carried the jewels in his arms, but Rachel and Kirsty could see that the hard shell of frost around them was already beginning to melt.

Jack Frost swooped down from the grey
sky and landed in the throne room of his
ice castle. By this time the frost around the
jewels had almost melted away. The jewels
glowed, casting shimmering rays of light
like laser beams into every corner of the
icy room. Goblins came running to see the
gems, wearing sunglasses to protect their
eyes from the glare.

"Stand back, you fools!" Jack Frost
roared, waving his wand again and

casting another spell to cover the
jewels with ice. But the jewels were still
glowing, and the ice began to melt away
almost immediately.

"Look, master," yelled one of the
goblins suddenly, "the fairy magic is
melting your castle!"

Jack Frost looked round in a fury. Sure
enough, water was beginning to trickle
down the icy walls, and there was a
puddle at the foot of his throne.

"Jack Frost's magic is not strong enough to block the power of the jewels," Queen Titania told Rachel and Kirsty.

The girls watched as the goblins began rushing around, mopping up the water as fast as they could. But as quickly as they cleared one puddle away, two more appeared.

"Very well then," shouted Jack Frost, stamping his feet in rage. "If I cannot keep these magic jewels, no one else shall have them! I will cast a spell to get rid of them." And he raised his wand high above his head.

Lost!

"Oh, no!" Kirsty gasped. She and Rachel watched in horror as an icy blast of wind whipped up around the throne room. The glowing jewels were sent spinning and tumbling across the room and out of the window, where they scattered far and wide.

"See how the jewels grow larger as
they fall into the human world?" Queen
Titania pointed out, just as the picture
in the pool began to flicker and fade.
"Because they are magical, they'll hide
themselves until we can find them and
bring them back to Fairyland."

The picture in the pool was fading
fast. But just before it disappeared,

Rachel saw one of the jewels, a creamy-coloured stone, fall into someone's back garden. With a start of surprise, Rachel realised that she knew exactly whose garden it was!

The Queen was shaking her head sadly as the picture vanished completely. "All of our fairy seeing magic is used up," she sighed. "So the pool can't show us where all the jewels have gone."

"But I know where one of them is!" Rachel burst out excitedly. "I recognised the garden where it fell!"

Everyone turned to stare at her.

"Are you sure, Rachel?" Kirsty asked.

Rachel nodded. "It was Mr and Mrs Palmer's back garden," she explained. "The Palmers are friends of my parents, and I've been to their house loads of times to help Mum babysit their little girl, Ellie."

One of the fairies was so excited at this that she whirled up into the air, her long brown hair streaming out behind her. "I'm India, the Moonstone Fairy," she cried, her eyes shining. "And I'm sure it was my Moonstone which fell into your friends' back garden!"

The little fairy wore a pretty dress with a nipped-in waist and floaty skirt.

The dress was white, but every time India moved, flashes of shimmering pink and blue shot through the material. On her feet she wore dainty white sandals.

"You must meet all our Jewel Fairies," said King Oberon, as the other fairies crowded around. "Each one is responsible for teaching all the other fairies how to use her jewel's magic." He pointed at India the Moonstone Fairy. "India teaches dream magic, while Emily the Emerald Fairy teaches seeing magic, Scarlett the Garnet Fairy teaches growing and shrinking magic, Chloe the Topaz Fairy teaches changing magic, Sophie the Sapphire Fairy teaches wishing magic, Amy the Amethyst Fairy teaches appearing and disappearing magic, and Lucy the Diamond Fairy teaches flying magic."

Rachel and Kirsty smiled round at all the fairies.

"We'll do our best to get your jewels back," Kirsty said.

"Thank you," the fairies replied.

"We knew you would help us," Queen Titania said gratefully. "But Jack Frost knows we will be trying to find the jewels, and he has sent his goblins into the human world to guard them."

"The goblins will find it difficult to pick the jewels up," King Oberon went on. "The bright light and magic of the gems will burn them, because they belong to the cold, icy world of Jack Frost. Instead, the goblins will probably lurk near the jewels and try to stop us getting them back."

Rachel and Kirsty nodded thoughtfully.

Queen Titania looked grave. "So now we need your help not only to find each magic jewel," she finished, "but also to outwit the goblins that will be guarding them!"

On the Right Track

"We'll find a way to get the jewels back," Rachel said firmly, and Kirsty nodded.

King Oberon smiled at them. "And you will have our Jewel Fairies to help you."

Rachel frowned. "I had a dream about the goblins chasing me," she said slowly.

India sighed,
looking very sad.
"Without the
Moonstone, the
fairies' power to
send sweet dreams
into the human
world is fading,"

she explained. "That's why you had a
nightmare, Rachel."

"India will return with you to your
world," said Queen Titania. "She'll help
you find the Moonstone."

"We know we have to look in the
Palmers' back garden," Kirsty said. "But
how will we know where to search for
the other jewels?"

Queen Titania smiled. "Just as before,
you must let the magic come to you,"

she replied. "The jewels will find you. And remember, they have grown bigger in the human world, so they will be easier to spot."

Rachel and Kirsty nodded. Then India fluttered over to join them and the Fairy Queen raised her wand.

"Good luck!" called the fairies, as the Queen waved her wand and Rachel, Kirsty and India disappeared in a shower of magic sparkles.

When the cloud of fairy dust vanished, Rachel and Kirsty realised that they were back in Rachel's bedroom.

"We must get to work right away, girls!" called a silvery voice.

The girls turned and saw India perched on the dressing-table mirror.

"Yes, let's go over to the Palmers' house now," said Rachel eagerly, making for the door.

Kirsty burst out laughing. "I think we'd better change out of our pyjamas first, don't you?"

"Good idea!" Rachel grinned.

"How can we get into the Palmers' back garden?" India asked, as the girls quickly got dressed.

"We could throw a ball over the fence," Kirsty suggested. "Then we could ask the Palmers if we can pop into their garden to find it."

"Yes, that would work," Rachel agreed.

"Girls, are you awake?" Mrs Walker's voice drifted up the stairs. "Breakfast's ready."

India fluttered across the room and hid

herself in Kirsty's pocket, and the girls hurried downstairs. "Mum," said Rachel, as she and Kirsty ate toast and jam, "is it OK if we go out to play after breakfast?"

"Yes," Mrs Walker agreed, "but don't go further than the park, and be back in time for lunch."

"Thanks, Mum." Rachel said, slipping out of her chair.

Kirsty did the same. "We need a ball," she whispered as they went to get their jackets.

"There's one in the shed, I think," Rachel replied.

The girls found a tennis ball and then set off down the road. Although it was autumn, it was quite a warm day and the sun shone down brightly from a blue sky.

"I hope my Moonstone is safe," India said softly, popping her head out of Kirsty's pocket. "I wonder if there are any goblins guarding it."

"We'll soon find out," Rachel replied, stopping in front of a house with a bright red door. "This is the Palmers' house."

The house was only three doors away from Rachel's home, on the corner of the street. Rachel took the ball out of her pocket, slipped round the corner and tossed it over the fence into the back garden. Then she joined Kirsty and India again in front of the house.

"I'll knock on the door," Rachel said, leading the way up the path.

"Let's hope they're in!" replied Kirsty.

Rachel rang the bell, and they waited for quite a while. Just as the girls and India were starting to give up hope, the door opened.

"Hello, Rachel," beamed Mrs Palmer. "And you must be Kirsty. Rachel told me she was having a friend to stay."

"Hello," Kirsty said politely.

"Sorry to disturb you, Mrs Palmer," Rachel said, "but I'm afraid we just lost our ball over your fence."

Mrs Palmer smiled. "As a matter of fact, I was just sitting in the back garden with Ellie. I didn't see your ball come over, though. Do you want to come and look for it?"

"Yes, please," Rachel replied.

"If you don't mind," added Kirsty.

Mrs Palmer opened the door wide. "Go straight through, girls. I'm just popping upstairs for a minute. Ellie's in her pram on the patio, if you want to say hello." Rachel led Kirsty through the kitchen and out through the back door.

India popped her head out of Kirsty's pocket. "The Moonstone's here somewhere," she cried happily. "I can feel it!"

"It's a big garden," Kirsty said. "We'd better start looking at once." She and India hurried over to the nearest flowerbed and began to peer among the shrubs. Meanwhile, Rachel went across the patio to say hello to Ellie. But as she walked towards the pram with its pretty white sunshade, Rachel began to shiver.

Suddenly there was a chill in the air.
A loud wail came from the pram.

Ellie had started to cry.
Ellie must be feeling
the cold, too, Rachel
thought. But it was
quite warm until
a moment ago!
Mrs Palmer rushed
out of the house and
ran over to the pram. "It's very
strange, Rachel," she said, as she
pushed back the sunshade and bent
down to pick up the baby. "Ellie's
always had trouble sleeping, but ever
since we got this mobile for her pram
yesterday, she's been sleeping ever so
well." Mrs Palmer frowned, lifting
Ellie out from under her lacy blanket.

"Something seems to be upsetting her today though; she's been very restless."

As Mrs Palmer picked Ellie up, the baby stretched out her chubby little hand to grab one of the decorations hanging from the mobile. Rachel looked at it more closely. It was hung with silver stars, yellow suns and pale moons. And then, suddenly, her heart missed a beat, for there, glittering in the middle of the mobile, was a cream-coloured stone which flashed with pink and blue light.

The Moonstone! Rachel thought excitedly. *No wonder Ellie's been sleeping well. She must have been having extra-sweet dreams!*

"I'm just going to take Ellie inside," said Mrs Palmer. "There's a chill in the air, all of a sudden."

"I hope that doesn't mean that some of Jack Frost's goblins are nearby," Rachel murmured to herself.

Leaving Mrs Palmer wrapping Ellie in a blanket, Rachel ran down the garden towards Kirsty and India, who were searching round the birdbath in the middle of the lawn.

"I've found the Moonstone!" Rachel whispered triumphantly. "It's hanging in the middle of the mobile on Ellie's pram."

"Wonderful!" India gasped.

"Well done, Rachel!" added Kirsty.

"Mrs Palmer's taking Ellie inside," said Rachel. "We can get the Moonstone as soon as she's gone."

The girls and India watched as Mrs Palmer carried Ellie into the house. Then Rachel and Kirsty immediately ran towards the pram, with India flying along beside them. But before they reached it, the door of the garden shed flew open with a crash, and two green goblins rushed out!

Hot Pursuit!

"The Moonstone is ours!" one of the goblins yelled. "And we'll never let the fairies have it back!"

"Never! Never!" shouted the other goblin.

As Kirsty, Rachel and India watched in horror, he leapt up onto the pram and grabbed at the string on which the

Moonstone was dangling.

"He's going to take the Moonstone!" Rachel gasped. "Stop him!"

As the girls rushed towards the pram, the other goblin panicked.

Hurriedly, he began pushing the pram off the patio, away from the girls. But the pram was much bigger than the goblin, who was only knee-high, and he couldn't control it properly. It bumped and bounced over the grass and onto the garden path. The goblin inside was caught off-balance.

With a screech of rage, he tumbled over
and got caught up in the
baby's blankets, before he
could grab the Moonstone.

Kirsty, Rachel and India
chased after the pram
as the goblin charged
down the garden path,
pushing it in front of
him. They could see
the Moonstone swinging
wildly on the mobile,
but they couldn't reach
it – the goblins were too far ahead.
The pram bounced and jolted its way
along, while the goblin inside was
struggling to free himself from the
tangle of blankets, and he shouted
crossly at his friend to stop.

Then, all of a sudden, one wheel hit
a large stone lying in the middle of the
path. The pram was going so fast that
it overturned. Both goblins let out shrill
cries of alarm as they flew through
the air. And then they both landed in
a heap, covered in Ellie's sheets and
blankets, underneath a large fir tree.

"India, can you stop
the goblins from
getting away?"
Kirsty panted,
as she and Rachel
chased down
the path towards
the goblins.

"I have a little
dream magic left
which might send the
goblins to sleep," India replied.
She zoomed ahead of the girls and
hovered over the goblins, waving her
wand. A few sparkles of fairy dust drifted
down onto the goblins, who stopped
struggling to free themselves
and began yawning and rubbing their
eyes instead.

"I'm so tired!" one of them sighed.

"And this blanket is really warm and cosy," the other one said sleepily. "I think I might have a little nap."

"Me too," the first goblin agreed. "Sing me a lullaby."

"No, you sing a lullaby!" the second goblin demanded.

"No, YOU!" yelled the first.

"They're waking themselves up with their silly argument!" Rachel exclaimed. "What are we going to do?"

"I think I have an idea!" Kirsty whispered, hurrying towards the goblins.

Rock-a-bye Goblins

Rachel and India watched as Kirsty began to tuck the goblins snugly into the blanket.

"Now, now, settle down," she said in a soft, sweet voice. "It's time for your nap."

The goblins stopped arguing and started yawning again.

"I am sleepy," the first goblin murmured, snuggling down under the pink blanket.

But the second goblin was trying hard to keep his eyes open. "Wasn't there something we were supposed to be doing?" he asked.

Rachel hurried over to help Kirsty. "Go to sleep now," she said in a soothing voice. "You can worry about that later."

And Kirsty began to sing a lullaby to
the tune of *Rock-a-bye Baby*:

"*Rock-a-bye Goblins wrapped in a rug,*
Asleep in the garden, all nice and snug,
When you wake up from your little nap,
You will find India's got her stone back."

By the second line of
Kirsty's little song, both
goblins were snoring
soundly.

"Well done, Kirsty,"
Rachel said with a grin.
"But we can't leave the
goblins here for Mrs Palmer
to find!"

"Leave that to me," India replied. She
waved her wand over a large branch
of the fir tree. Immediately, the branch
drooped lower, so that the leaves

completely covered the sleeping goblins.

"Perfect!" Kirsty declared. "The goblins are green like the leaves, so they'll be well hidden until they wake up."

India and Rachel laughed.

"Then they'll have to rush back to Jack Frost and tell him they've lost the Moonstone," India said. "They'll be in big trouble!"

Chuckling quietly, the girls picked up the
pram and pushed it back to
the patio. Then, as India
watched in delight,
Kirsty carefully
took the magic
Moonstone from
the middle
of the mobile.
It flashed and
gleamed in
the sunlight.

"We mustn't spoil
Ellie's mobile," India said.
She waved her wand and a
glittering, shiny bubble appeared in
place of the Moonstone on the mobile.

As it caught the light, it sent
rainbow-colours shining in all directions.

"And now," India went on, "the Moonstone is going straight back to Fairyland and the Queen's tiara, where it belongs!" She touched her wand to the jewel. Immediately a fountain of sparkling fairy dust shot up into the air and the Moonstone vanished.

"Thank you, girls," India said, giving Rachel and Kirsty a hug. "I must go home now, but I hope you'll be able to help the other Jewel Fairies find their magic stones too."

"We'll do our best!" Rachel promised.

"Goodbye, India!" Kirsty added, as their fairy friend flew away in a cloud of sparkles.

"I wonder where the other six jewels are hiding," Rachel murmured.

"And I wonder if we'll have to face many more goblins," Kirsty said with a frown.

Rachel shivered, remembering her nightmare. "I just hope I don't dream about them again tonight," she said.

Kirsty laughed. "Don't worry, Rachel," she told her friend. "India's got the Moonstone back now; she's sure to send you sweet dreams!"

**Now Rachel and Kirsty
must help...**

Scarlett the Garnet Fairy

Read on for a sneak peek...

"Wakey, wakey!" Rachel Walker called,
bouncing on the end of her friend Kirsty's
bed. Kirsty Tate was staying with the
Walker family for the October half-term
holiday and Rachel didn't want to waste
a single second.

Kirsty yawned and stretched. "I just had
the most amazing dream," she said sleepily.
"Queen Titania asked us to help the Jewel
Fairies find seven stolen gemstones from
her magic tiara and..." Her voice trailed
away and she opened her eyes wide. "It
wasn't a dream, was it?" she said, sitting

bolt upright. "We really did meet India the Moonstone Fairy yesterday!"

Rachel nodded, smiling. "We certainly did," she agreed. Kirsty and Rachel shared a wonderful secret. They were friends with the fairies! They had had all sorts of fantastic adventures with them in the past – and now the fairies were in trouble. Mean Jack Frost had stolen the seven magical jewels from the Fairy Queen's tiara. He had wanted to keep the jewels for himself, but their magic was so powerful that his ice castle had begun to melt. In a rage, Jack Frost had hurled the jewels away, and now they were lost.

King Oberon and Queen Titania had asked the girls to help return the jewels to Fairyland. Yesterday, Kirsty and

Rachel had helped India the Moonstone Fairy find the magic Moonstone. But there were still six jewels left to find...

Read Scarlett the Garnet Fairy
to find out what adventures are in store for Kirsty and Rachel!

Meet the
Jewel Fairies

Join Rachel and Kirsty as they hunt for the
jewels that naughty Jack Frost has stolen
from Queen Titania's crown!

www.rainbowmagicbooks.co.uk

Calling all parents, carers and teachers!
The Rainbow Magic fairies are here to help
your child enter the magical world of reading.
Whatever reading stage they are at, there's
a Rainbow Magic book for everyone!
Here is Lydia the Reading Fairy's guide to
supporting your child's journey at all levels.

Starting Out

 1

Our Rainbow Magic Beginner Readers are perfect for first-time readers who are just beginning to develop reading skills and confidence. Approved by teachers, they contain a full range of educational levelling, as well as lively full-colour illustrations.

Developing Readers

2

Rainbow Magic Early Readers contain longer stories and wider vocabulary for building stamina and growing confidence. These are adaptations of our most popular Rainbow Magic stories, specially developed for younger readers in conjunction with an Early Years reading consultant, with full-colour illustrations.

Going Solo

3

The Rainbow Magic chapter books - a mixture of series and one-off specials - contain accessible writing to encourage your child to venture into reading independently. These highly collectible and much-loved magical stories inspire a love of reading to last a lifetime.

www.rainbowmagicbooks.co.uk

"Rainbow Magic got my daughter reading chapter books. Great sparkly covers, cute fairies and traditional stories full of magic that she found impossible to put down" - Mother of Edie (6 years)

"Florence LOVES the Rainbow Magic books. She really enjoys reading now" Mother of Florence (6 years)

The Rainbow Magic Reading Challenge

Well done, fairy friend – you have completed the book!
This book was worth 5 points.

See how far you have climbed on the **Reading Rainbow** on the Rainbow Magic website below.

The more books you read, the more points you will get, and the closer you will be to becoming a Fairy Princess!

How to get your Reading Rainbow
1. Cut out the coin below
2. Go to the Rainbow Magic website
3. Download and print out your poster
4. Add your coin and climb up the Reading Rainbow!

There's all this and lots more at
www.rainbowmagicbooks.co.uk

You'll find activities, competitions, stories, a special newsletter and complete profiles of all the Rainbow Magic fairies. Find a fairy with your name!